Miss Hoot

Mole

Frog

Mouse

Owl

Rabbit

For Gracie
LM

First published 2019 by Macmillan Children's Books
an imprint of Pan Macmillan
20 New Wharf Road, London N1 9RR
Associated companies throughout the world
www.panmacmillan.com

ISBN 978-1-5098-8149-9

Text and illustrations copyright © Lydia Monks 2019

1 3 5 7 9 8 6 4 2

A CIP catalogue record for this book is available
from the British Library.

Printed in China

Rabbit
Races Ahead!

MACMILLAN CHILDREN'S BOOKS

It was a special day at Twit Twoo School, and all the children were very excited. It was Sports Day!

They had been training all week, especially Rabbit. She had decided that she was going to win every single race!

Mouse was really good at running, but Rabbit was faster.

Owl was great at long jump, but Rabbit could jump further.

Frog was fantastic
at jumping high, but
Rabbit always beat him.

Mole was trying to get
the hang of skipping, but
Rabbit was an expert.

"I'm the best! I'm going to win every race, just watch me!" boasted Rabbit.

"She's such a show-off!" muttered Mouse to Mole.

"She's not being very kind!" whispered Owl to Frog,
as they went to have a sit down and a drink.

No one wanted to sit with Rabbit.

"Come on everyone!" called Miss Hoot.
"It's time for the first race!"

They started with the running race.
Mouse ran really fast, but Rabbit came first.

Then it was the long jump. Owl jumped
a long way, but Rabbit came first.

Next it was the high jump. Frog's bounce was super, but Rabbit came first.

The skipping race was next. Mole made a great effort . . . but Rabbit came first.

"See, I told you I'd win!" laughed Rabbit. She was a bit surprised that the others didn't seem very pleased for her.

The children left Rabbit to admire her medals.

"Miss Hoot, they're all being mean to me!" complained Rabbit.

"Maybe try to think about other people's feelings," replied Miss Hoot. "I'm sure they're pleased you've won, but they might be a bit sad that they didn't win anything themselves."

Miss Hoot made an announcement. It was time for the very last race of the day – the long distance race!

"Two times around the wood," she called. "On your marks, get set, GO!"

Rabbit got off to a flying start. She was soon out of sight.
She ran so fast that she finished her first lap in record time,
and was beginning to catch up with the others.

Rabbit ran around the bend and came across
Mouse, who was crying. Mouse had got scared
being on her own in the deep dark wood.

"Would you like to carry on running with me?" asked Rabbit.
"I don't want to!" sobbed Mouse.

Rabbit took Mouse by the paw, and led her back to Miss Hoot.

Rabbit set off again. She'd been so far ahead, she was sure she could still win. But it wasn't long before she bumped into Owl. He had fallen over and hurt his knee.

"Are you all right?" asked Rabbit.
"I want my mummy!" sobbed Owl.

Rabbit took Owl by the wing, and
led him back to Miss Hoot too.

Rabbit went back to the race, sprinting as fast as she could. As she ran along, she heard some rustling in the bushes. She could see Frog's head popping up and down!

"Are you lost?" called Rabbit.
"Yes, I tried to find a short cut," shouted Frog,
"but it hasn't worked!"

Rabbit rescued Frog, and made sure
he hopped off in the right direction.

Rabbit bounded on up the path, and nearly
tripped over something. It was Mole.
He was so worn out that he'd sat down for a rest.

"Are you okay?" asked Rabbit.
"I can't do this!" panted Mole.
"I'm rubbish at running!"

"Have a little rest, then
we'll carry on together.
I'll help you!" said Rabbit.

After a few minutes, Mole felt better.
Rabbit took his paw, and they ran off together.

Rabbit went as slowly as she could, which was hard for her. She knew she wouldn't win the race now, but she felt sorry for Mole.

There was the finish line up ahead! She was about to sprint off, but then she changed her mind.

"Go on Mole, you can do it!" smiled Rabbit, as she let go of his paw.

Mole had won the race, and Rabbit had come last!
"Well done Mole!" cried Miss Hoot, handing him a medal.

"And well done Rabbit, who I think
deserves a special cheer for being so kind."
"Hooray!" they all shouted.

Rabbit was so proud. It felt good to be kind.
Even better than coming first.

"I think you all deserve an ice-cream," said Miss Hoot.
And everyone wanted to sit with Rabbit!

Miss Hoot

Mole

Frog

Mouse

Owl

Rabbit